BOY SOUP

or
When Giant Caught Cold

Written and illustrated
by Loris Lesynski

Annick Press
Toronto New York

Third printing, January 1998

Annick Press Ltd.

CANADA COUNCIL | LE CONSEIL DES ARTS
FOR THE ARTS | DU CANADA
SINCE 1957 | DEPUIS 1957

We acknowledge the support of the Canada Council
for the Arts for our publishing program.
We also thank the Ontario Arts Council.

Cataloguing in Publication Data

Lesynski, Loris
  Boy soup, or, When giant caught cold

ISBN 1-55037-417-6 (bound)   ISBN 1-55037-416-8 (pbk.)

I. Title. II. Title: When giant caught cold.

PS8573.E79B69 1996   jC813'.54   C96-930569-9
PZ7.L47Bo 1996

The art in this book was rendered in watercolour and coloured pencil.
The text was typeset in Utopia.

Distributed in Canada by: Published in the U.S.A. by Annick Press (U.S.) Ltd.
  Firefly Books Ltd.   Distributed in the U.S.A. by:
  3680 Victoria Park Avenue   Firefly Books (U.S.) Inc.
  Willowdale, ON   P.O. Box 1338
  M2H 3K1   Ellicott Station
                                     Buffalo, NY 14205

Printed on acid-free paper.

Printed and bound in Canada
by Friesens, Altona, Manitoba.

To "The Goup"

Giant woke up with a big hurting head.
"I am sore I am sick I feel awful," he said.

He coughed—
    moving mountains.
He hacked—
    causing quakes.
He said, with a whimper,
    "My everything aches."
Groaning, he shovelled his blankets aside,
and reached for his *Giants' Home Medical Guide.*

With sofa-sized fingers,
   he leafed through the book,
and in between sneezes
   so loud that he shook,
he found all his symptoms—
   page seventy-one:

   "Queasiness,
   wheeziness,
   coughing begun.
   Completely depleted,
   and tending to droop."

The only prescription?

A bowl of
Boy Soup.

"Can't *be*," said the giant. "Would be a disgrace."
But a big greedy grin spread all over his face.

"Of course—if I'm ill—that's a decent excuse.
  And think of the broth
        a good boy could produce.
A sweet boy, a neat boy,
  a boy so delicious
        a giant might find himself
            licking the dishes…
One *buttery* boy, or better—a group!
  A half-dozen lads would make
        wonderful soup!"

Catching the boys was as easy as pie:
  he stretched down his thick giant
    arm through the sky
      and rested his hand at the top of a tree
        where children were playing.
          They just didn't see—
            the branch they were grabbing
              could grab *them*.
                Too late!

That's how the giant got five boys—
and Kate.

" Why *should* I
feel guilty—"
the giant began,
when six angry children
protested his plan.

"—It's here in this
authorized medical book!"

Kate asked, "Before supper,
could *I* have a look?"

She read every word
in the faded ink
and said, "May I have
just a minute to think?"

—but *"No!"* snapped the giant. "Boys, *into* the pot!
I've chills and a fever,
I'm cold and I'm hot."
And then with a thunderous splat blew his nose
as the boys shook with fear
from their heads to their toes.

Kate racked her brain at a furious rate
to save all her friends from this hideous fate.
The giant was ready.
Oh, *how* could they flee?

Their ten rubber running shoes—
that was the key!

Just as the giant came closer to scoop
the lads for his horrid medicinal soup,
Kate gave a signal, the tiniest look.
The boys understood. They leapt to the book
and started a dance, half a shuffle, half-run,
and jogged back and forth
on page seventy-one.
Up the page, down the page
sidestep, repeat—

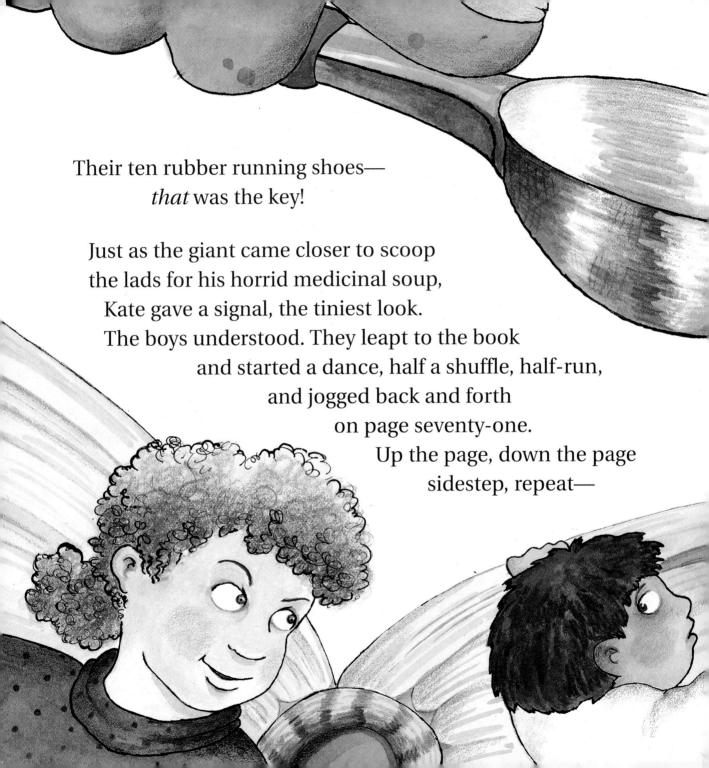

'til most
of each word
was erased
by their feet.

"Now I can't check it!"
  the giant complained.
  But Kate said, "I've read it,
  I'll gladly explain.
  The book said quite clearly—
  of this I am sure—
  Boy Soup is soup
  made by boys,
  that's the cure."

"But . . ." sniffed the giant,
"I thought boys went *in* it . . .
  I think I'm confused . . .
  can you give me a minute?"

"Oh, no," Kate proclaimed,
"you're too sick, don't you know.
  We have to work fast.
  Come on, fellows, let's go!"

The boys cooked the carrots ✔
    the boys boiled the peas ✔
then seasoned the soup with
    a handful of fleas. ✔

They put in
    some mud ✔
    and some thick yellow glue ✔
    and a generous dollop of dandruff shampoo. ✔

Kate poured in
    pepper ✔
    and red hot sauce ✔
    rotten bananas ✔
    and candy floss ✔
    sour green pickles ✔
    and beans in the can ✔
—all simmered together as part of the plan.

    And oh, the aroma!
    Like skunk in a pot.

    Kate smiled her sweetest
      —and served it up hot.

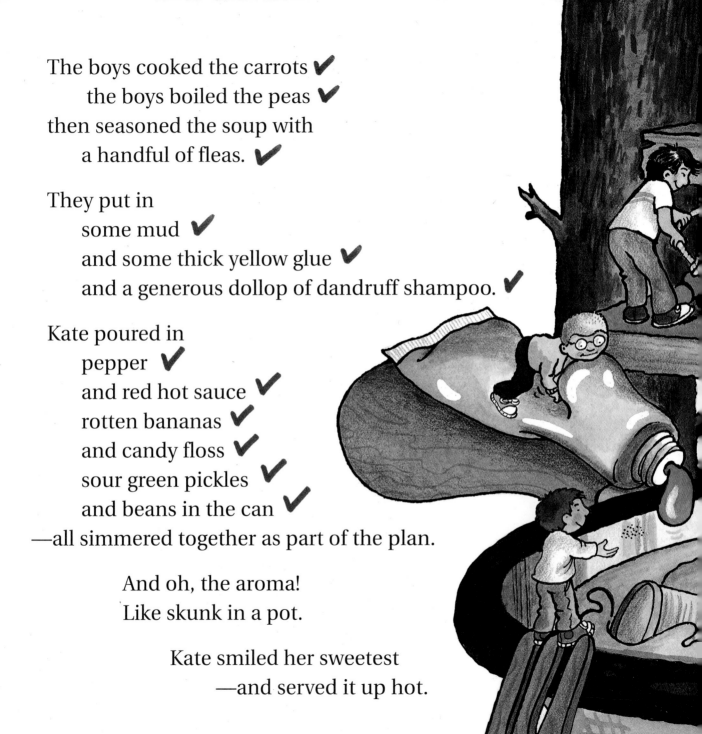

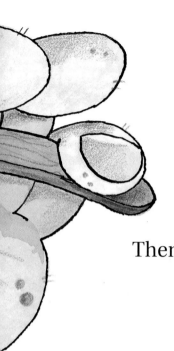

In between snuffles, the giant took sips
from a spoon trembling close
to his great hairy lips.

He scowled in suspicion but took one more taste,
with a huge doughy tongue
much the colour of paste—

Then tipped the whole potful of soup down his throat
. . . sat back . . .
and *sighed*—

'til he started to bloat!
—and the pepper, the mud, and the pickles combined.
The giant let out a most terrible whine—

and SPIT out the soup with so mighty a blast

that it blew

all the children

down homeward at last.

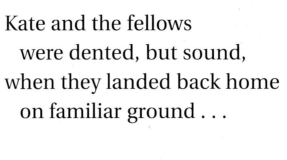

Kate and the fellows
were dented, but sound,
when they landed back home
on familiar ground . . .

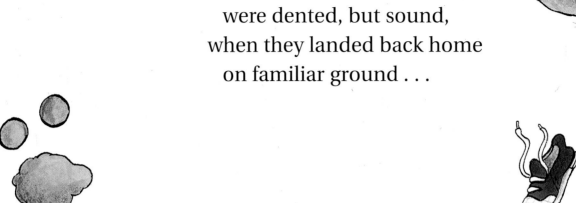

They needed new sneakers,
    and something to do
to get over the horrible shock
    they'd been through.

The giant was not
    who they wanted to feed,
but they *had* liked the cooking,
    with Kate in the lead.

They opened "Boys' Restaurant"
    —as a group—
—and served almost everything
    but Boy Soup.

One day at the diner, delivery came
of an extra-large envelope bearing Kate's name.
The giant had written:

I did get your letter.
    Thank you for asking,
        I <u>am</u> feeling better.

That Medical Book is from long, long ago.
They boiled little boys then —
    even though
you're right that it's wrong.
    I guess that I knew it.
But feeling so sick made me
    tempted to do it.

I'm glad that you tricked me —
    I would have felt bad
    when later I realized
    I'd eaten a lad.
    I told all the giants:
    No boy soup for me!

Sorry again,

Yours sincerely,
Big G.